but I know she still loves me.

My mum goes to work,
but I know she still cares about me.

My Mum Goes to Work

Written by
Kes Gray

Illustrated by
David Milgrim

Hodder
Children's
Books

a division of Hachette Children's Books

My mum goes to work,

My mum goes to work,
but I know she still thinks about me all the time.

I know she'd like to be cuddling me.

I know she'd like to be tickling me.

I know she'd like to be playing games with me . . .

drawing with me . . .

bike riding with me . . .

rollerblading with me ...

painting pictures with me ...

My mum goes to work,
but I know she'd like
to be pushing me
on my swing.

How do I know?

Because my mum comes home from work!

And when
she does,
she tells
me she
loves me
SO MUCH . . .

tickles me **SO MUCH** . . .

bike rides with me SO MUCH...

rollerblades with me SO MUCH. . .

paints with me **SO MUCH** . . .

and pushes me
on my swing

SO MUCH . . .

For my wife Claire, the hardest
working mum I know. K.G

For Kendra. D.M

MY MUM GOES TO WORK
Written by Kes Gray
Illustrated by David Milgrim

British Library Cataloguing in Publication Data
A catalogue record of this book is available
from the British Library.

ISBN: 978 0340 88369 3 (PB)

First published 2006.
Paperback edition first published 2007.

10 9 8 7 6 5 4 3 2 1

Published by Hodder Children's Books,
a division of Hachette Children's Books,
338 Euston Road, London, NW1 3BH

Hodder Children's Books Australia,
Hachette Children's Books,
Level 17/207 Kent Street
Sydney, NSW 2000

Printed in China